READ ALL THE SPARKLE PIGS BOOKS!

SPARKLY SPOTLIGHT

written by
KIT HOLLIDAY

illustrated by
DIZZY DEVIL DESIGNS

HARPER
An Imprint of HarperCollins*Publishers*

To Ava, the sparkliest star I know

Special thanks to Stephanie Campisi

Sparkle Pigs #3: Sparkly Spotlight
Copyright © 2025 by Working Partners Ltd.
All rights reserved. Manufactured in Crawfordsville, IN, United States of America. No part of this book may be used or reproduced in any manner whatsoever without written permission except in the case of brief quotations embodied in critical articles and reviews. For information address HarperCollins Children's Books, a division of HarperCollins Publishers, 195 Broadway, New York, NY 10007.
www.harpercollinschildrens.com

Library of Congress Control Number: 2024948633
ISBN 978-0-06-332342-1

24 25 26 27 28 LBC 5 4 3 2 1
First Edition

CONTENTS

1: Muffin and the Extremely Official Invitation.. 1
2: Ziggy and the Hard-to-Narrow-Down Talent!! 7
3: Muffin and the Very Broad Definition of "Talent" 16
4: Ziggy and the Bunniest Trick Ever!!............... 23
5: Muffin and the Bad Hare Day........................31
6: Ziggy and the Most Delicious Password!! 36
7: Muffin and the Dignified Search Party 43
8: Ziggy and the Castle Karaoke Singer!! 49
9: Muffin and the Case of Unmistakable Identity... 54
10: Ziggy and the Master of Disguise!! 59
11: Muffin and the End of the Bunny Business....65
12: Ziggy and the Grand Finale!! 75
13: Muffin and the Perfectly Piggie Ending......... 83

1
MUFFIN AND THE EXTREMELY OFFICIAL INVITATION

Muffin puffed up with pride. The hutch was so clean it *sparkled*. She could see her reflection in the polished plastic water bottle!

It made her want to *sing*! However, Ziggy was still sleeping, and Muffin didn't want to wake her. But she could recite a poem. A poem had never woken anyone.

"Oh, I am a tidy piggie," whispered Muffin.
"I polish, scrub, and clean.

"Turning sloppy into spotless,
"I am a hygiene queen!"
But then.
Scuff, scuff. Scratch, scratch. Crinkle, crinkle!
Oh no.
YAWN.
Here it came.
BOMP! THWACK! WHUMP!
No. Just no. Ziggy was not going to ruin Muffin's freshly tidied floor! Muffin flattened

herself against the shredded paper, trying to protect it.

But there was no stopping Ziggy.

"MUFFIN!" squealed Ziggy, whirling into the main hutch area like a fluffy tornado. Shredded paper exploded everywhere.

Muffin wanted to cry.

"I had the most INCREDIBLE dream!" continued Ziggy. "I was doing the most AMAZING dance! Ready to see it?"

Muffin was never ready for these things.

Ziggy bounced and flipped and spun. It was a bit like when Jackson, one of their humans, tried out new tricks on his skateboard. (At least *he* wore a helmet.)

Muffin took a deep breath. This was fine. Everything was fine. Just more to tidy later! Lots more, in fact!

"Are you grinding your teeth in time with my dance?" asked Ziggy.

"It stops them from growing too long," replied Muffin cheerily. (Muffin was an excellent actor.)

"Well, you make a FABULOUS percussion instrument!"

"Thank you, Ziggy. I'm . . . going to trim the grass outside now."

But as Muffin turned away, a bright light began to glow at the edge of her vision. She blinked.

Either Ziggy had chewed a hole in the hutch or . . .

"MUFFIN! MUFFIN! The Piggie-Town door is back! And I just got whacked on the head with a ticket! TWO tickets!"

In spite of the Piggie-Town door's terrible timing, Muffin couldn't resist. Tickets were so *official*! Muffin loved official things.

Even when they said things like:

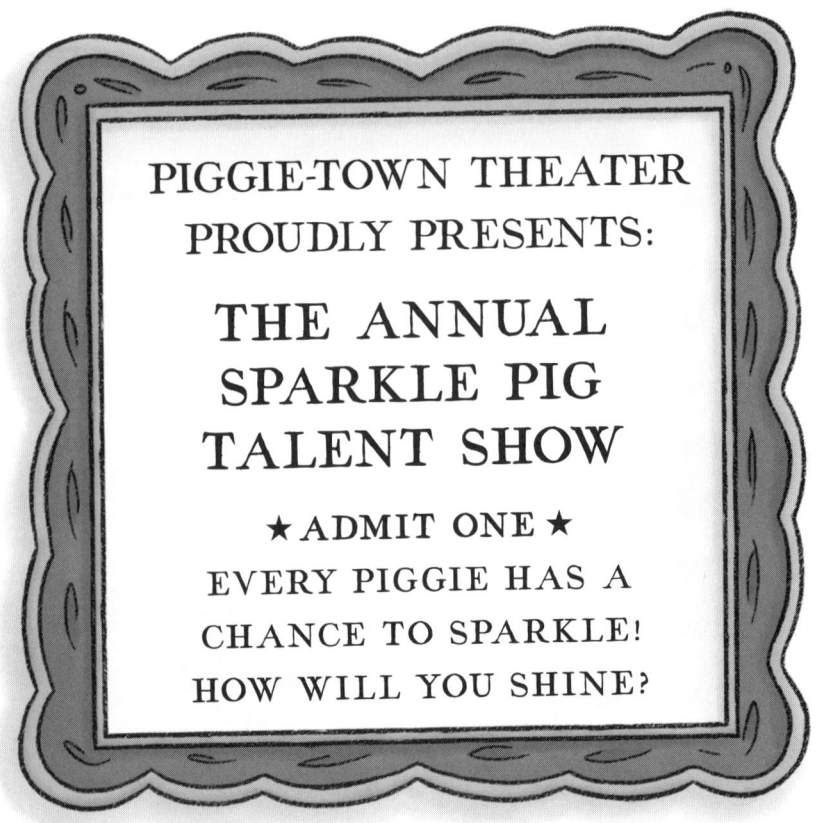

2

ZIGGY AND THE HARD-TO-NARROW-DOWN TALENT!!

A talent show! Ziggy loved talent shows. The problem was that she had too many talents to choose from!

"I could play my trumpet flower!" she mused. "Or pat my head while rubbing my belly! Ooh! What about unpeeling a mandarin in a single spiral! Or all those at the same time! Muffin, how do I choose?"

"I'm glad you have so many talents, Ziggy."

Muffin straightened a piece of bedding, then sighed. "I don't even have one."

Ziggy blinked. Muffin was the most talented piggie Ziggy had ever met! "But you're a cleaning superstar! A tidying *champion*!"

"Tidying isn't a proper talent," replied Muffin. "It's just something I do."

But Ziggy had LOTS more talents to list. "You can organize *anything*, even ME! And just a few weeks back, you led all the Sparkle Pigs in the most incredible parade!"

"That's true," admitted Muffin.

"I believe in you, Muffin! Even more than I believe in Bigfoot!"

Ziggy grabbed Muffin's paw and pulled her through the glowing doorway. There was that gloriously wonky feeling of being yanked in all directions and then . . .

PLOP!

What a fabulous entrance! (Ziggy had a special talent for entrances!)

But not as fabulous as the entrance to the Piggie-Town Theater, where they'd landed. The doorway bloomed with ruffly kale arrangements. There was even a huge sign lit with hollowed-out turnip bulbs!

All around them, the Sparkle Pigs . . . well, *sparkled*! They dripped with jewels and sequins and shimmery fabric. They looked so glamorous and fancy!

Did this mean . . . Yes! Yes, it did!

Ziggy popcorned and twisted, trying to see her outfit. A sparkly top hat and tails! Ziggy *loved* top hats!

"Thank you, Piggie-Town!" she squeaked.

"I've worn worse," said Muffin, who was in a MAGNIFICENT evening gown. It had puffy shoulders, gloves (not puffy), and a little purse, perfect for carrying a single strawberry!

"Do come in!" cried a piggie usher (also very well dressed). "Take some popcorn, take some ice cream, and most important, take your seats!"

"Take them where?" asked Ziggy.

"He means sit down," said Muffin.

"Are you sure?" asked Ziggy. But she found an empty spot and plunked her bottom on it.

Squeak! went the seat.

Ziggy squealed in excitement.

"Muffin! Muffin! These seats go up and down!"

She climbed off.

Up!

She climbed on.

Down!

"Ziggy," warned Muffin. "If you keep doing that, you'll break the chair."

The kindly looking elderly piggie next to Ziggy chuckled. She was dressed in a white uniform cinched with a black belt, like the one Sophia, their other human, wore on weekends.

"Are you . . . a karate piggie?" asked Ziggy.

"I am," said the piggie. "My name is Granny Pig, although some call me the Kitchen Ninja. I can chop vegetables with my bare paws. Watch."

THWACK!

Granny Pig attacked Muffin's popcorn with an outstretched paw. A blizzard of popcorn fragments went flying. It was like being in a popcorn snow globe!

"Wow," said Muffin. Her eye twitched.

"Muffin, let's try it when we get home. We'll chop *everything*!" Ziggy cried.

"Oh good," said Muffin, who was down on the carpet picking up popcorn.

"Home?" Granny Pig considered this. "Oh! You mean you're from the People Place. Like Fred! I do hope he makes it tonight. He performs the most hilarious songs about rutabagas!"

Granny Pig snorted at the thought. So did Ziggy. Rutabagas! Even the name was silly.

"I can't wait to finally meet Fred!" exclaimed Ziggy. "We've heard so much about him!"

"Shhh!" said Muffin. "It's starting!"

"BRAVO!" shouted Ziggy.

"Not yet, Ziggy," said Muffin.

A furry leg kicked open the theater curtain and an extremely fluffy piggie pranced across the stage. Then she struck the most *fabulous* pose.

"That's Fluffina," said Granny Pig. "She's a showpiggie."

Ziggy was awestruck. Fluffina was so COOL.

"Ladies and gentlepigs!" cried Fluffina into a carrot microphone. "Welcome to the Sparkle Pig Talent Show! We have a sparklerific lineup for you tonight! There'll be cake decorating.

There'll be lettuce carving. And most of all, there'll be *magic*. And now, without further ado . . ." Fluffina paused for dramatic effect.

A sign lit up behind her.

"It's time to shine!" shouted the piggies in unison.

You've read TWO chapters . . . off to a SPARKLY start!

3

MUFFIN AND THE VERY BROAD DEFINITION OF "TALENT"

Muffin couldn't believe her eyes. Or rather, she hoped she couldn't. She was no expert on talent shows, but should they involve *quite* so much chaos?

They'd already endured a ventriloquist piggie with an oddly silent parsnip puppet. Then vegetable balloon tying (it had not gone well). Then a piggie chess pro who claimed he could play seven games of chess at once.

Unfortunately, none of the other Sparkle Pigs knew the rules. (And Muffin had been too shy to put up her paw.)

And now . . .

"Let's give a warm piggie welcome for Piggie-Town's number one carrot-grower AND carrot-thrower . . . Chatter!" cried Fluffina.

All right. This didn't sound so bad. Muffin liked carrots, and she liked Chatter as well. But why was there a piggie tied to a spinning wheel at the far end of the stage?

Oh no. Chatter was going to throw carrots at his poor captive assistant!

Muffin buried her face in a puffy sleeve as the carrots went flying.

"Tell me when it's safe to look," she whispered.

"She's catching them *in her mouth*!" Ziggy leaped up and down in her seat. "She's eating them!"

"That's my kind of trick," said Granny Pig.

"Muffin! Muffin!" shouted Ziggy. "He's upgrading to asparagus spears!"

Muffin squeezed her eyes closed, only opening them again when the whole theater started to rumble.

Was that an earthquake?

"IT'S BIG PIG!" shrieked Ziggy.

They'd met Big Pig—sort of—during the Piggie Parade last time they'd been here. Big Pig was a capybara with a special talent for sleeping in challenging conditions.

Big Pig was too big to fit through the theater doors. Instead, he poked his head through a specially made window near stage right.

He nodded timidly at the audience, then burst into an operatic aria so intense that it literally knocked everyone's hats off.

"PHENOMENAL!" declared Ziggy, reaching for her top hat.

"Ah, *The Marriage of Pigaro*," whispered Granny Pig. "Have you ever heard anything like it?"

Muffin hadn't. Especially the part where Big Pig forgot the words and had to improvise. Luckily, all the other pigs helped him out.

After Big Pig came a tap-dancing troupe dressed head to paw in blue sequins.

"We're the Blueberries!" announced the head piggie. "And we've worked berry hard on our routine!"

Muffin wasn't sure that the hard work had paid off. The Blueberries' routine was a fruit salad of mistimed high-kicks and spins that was meant to finish with a piggie pyramid. Unfortunately, the pyramid collapsed into a piggie pile.

"Crushed it!" grunted one of the Blueberries.

"Literally!" added Fluffina, helping him up.

"BRILLIANT! Did you see that, Granny Pig?" squealed Ziggy, as the Blueberries somersaulted offstage. "Wait, where did you go?"

Moments later, the spotlights came back on.

Granny Pig bowed her head, then flexed her paws.

Chop! Thwack! Smack!

Vegetables went flying.

"Dinner is served!" cried Fluffina, catching some cabbage in one paw. (Now there was a  talent, Muffin thought to herself.) "I think that's a good time for an intermission and veggie break, don't you? But stick around, because when we come back . . . it's time for the Wiz Pig's Fantabulous Magic Trick!"

Muffin sighed. Oh joy. Magic.

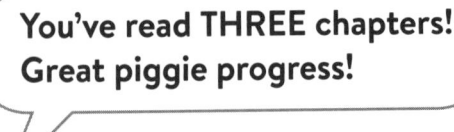

You've read THREE chapters! Great piggie progress!

4

ZIGGY AND THE BUNNIEST TRICK EVER!!

OH JOY. MAGIC!!

Was it possible to turn inside out from excitement? Just when Ziggy thought the talent show couldn't get any better, someone was about to do MAGIC? She munched her toffee apple in excitement.

"Ziggy!" came a chorus of voices from behind her. It was the Sparkle Pigs from the band she'd played in during the Piggie Parade!

"Fancy seeing you here!"

A REUNION! Ziggy loved reunions. "I have the BEST song for you!" she squealed.

Trumpet flowers honked and cucumber-leles twanged as Ziggy taught the band piggies the song from her dream.

It sounded even better in real life!!

"That concludes the intermission, Sparkle Pigs!" called Fluffina. "Please return to your seats!"

"Thanks for the jam session, Ziggy!" called the piggie band trombonist.

There was chaos as the Sparkle Pigs tried to remember where they'd been sitting.

Fortunately Muffin's puffed sleeves were easy to spot. Ziggy rushed along the aisle and plonked herself down. She squirmed in her chair.

"Ziggy," whispered Muffin. "Did you forget to use the . . . *bathroom?*"

"This is EXCITED squirming, Muffin! HERE HE IS!"

As the last few Sparkle Pigs hurried to their seats, the theater lights dimmed. The usher piggies wafted dandelion fluff around like smoke.

Oh. Boy. The. Anticipation.

A spotlight snapped on, revealing a mysterious cloaked figure in a wonky wizard's hat.

Ziggy clapped her paws over her mouth, trying to push a squeak back in. (Too late!) This was so thrilling! And that hat! She'd never seen such a magical hat!

The Wiz Pig blinked, then laughed nervously. "Oh wow, that's quite a crowd. I haven't been around this many piggies in a while . . ."

He paused. It looked like he was counting, the way Muffin sometimes did after Ziggy made an especially funny joke!

After a few seconds, the Wiz Pig clapped his paws and bowed—he was ready.

Ziggy was on the edge of her seat.

The Wiz Pig gave a theatrical flap of his cloak. A table appeared!

"AMAZING!" squealed Ziggy.

"That . . . wasn't the trick," said the Wiz Pig. "But thank you."

"He spoke to me!" squealed Ziggy. "He looked confusedly in our direction!"

Another cloak flap. Now the Wiz Pig's hat was on the table! (Along with some lovely flowers.)

"Tonight I will attempt a trick of never-before-seen difficulty. I will pull a rabbit out of this hat!"

"Not a chance," muttered Muffin. "That hat is far too small."

The Wiz Pig raised his wand.

"Is that . . . a celery stalk?" whispered Muffin.

"SHHH!" shushed Ziggy.

"Pig-wiggery-ki-dibbery!" recited the Wiz Pig.

FLASH!

The theater glowed the deep purple of blackberry juice.

"Ooooh!" cried the audience. "Aaaah!"

"What a tremendous achievement!" called Chatter from the front row.

"You get my vote!" cried Granny Pig.

"But there's no rabbit," pointed out Muffin. "Shouldn't there be a rabbit?"

"Muffin," said Ziggy, "magic isn't about results! It's about DRAMA! ILLUSIONS!

MISDIRECTION!"

She leaped to her paws, ready to applaud.

BOING!

Oops, she'd bounced all the way up to the ceiling! But how?

"Something's not right," said Muffin, from way below. She looked very odd. Was it the angle? No! It was because she had . . . bunny feet and bunny ears and bunny teeth!

Ziggy whooped (and bounced). She was

a bunny, too! So was Granny Pig, who was practicing karate kicks with her powerful bunny back legs. And Fluffina, who was wincing at her bunny teeth in a compact mirror.

EVERYONE was a bunny!

This was, paws down, the best talent Ziggy had ever seen!!

You've read FOUR chapters! Way to go!

5

MUFFIN AND THE BAD HARE DAY

Muffin was not having a good time. It was *impossible* to sit comfortably with a bunny tail, and she could hardly see past these floppy ears. She would not put up with this one second longer!

"WA-HEE!" cried Scooter, the Piggie-Town train conductor. He was bouncing about without the slightest consideration for anyone's safety!

In fact, *none* of the Sparkle Pigs were following basic safety rules! There were feet on seats!

Ears in the popcorn!

It was chaos. Mayhem. Pandemonium!

Trying to keep her new feet beneath her, Muffin bounded over to the Wiz Pig. Of course, *he* hadn't been transformed into a bunny. How convenient.

"Mr. Wiz Pig! This isn't funny! We're breaking every rule and regulation of all good theaters! We're a *fire hazard*! Turn us back right now!"

The Wiz Pig seemed to shrink under her gaze. (Good!)

"Muffin! MUFFIN!" Ziggy came leaping over, clearing three rows of seats at a time. "Are you going up on stage? Let's go up together! We can do a hip-hop dance!"

No way, no how. This was out of the question.

Muffin awkwardly folded her paws. "I'm asking the Wiz Pig to return us to our piggie selves."

The Wiz Pig wrapped his cloak around himself. "About that. I'm not *exactly* sure what happened. I really did mean to pull a rabbit out of my hat. But I can fix it. Absolutely. I'll do it right now."

The Wiz Pig pulled out his celery stick wand and waved it purposefully around. "Piggie-wee-dazzle-donk!"

FLASH!

Lightning crackled once more, and the auditorium filled with lavender-colored smoke. (It smelled quite refreshing.)

But when it cleared . . .

Disaster. Not only were the Sparkle Pigs still bunnies, but they were even *more* bunny-like. They were bouncing higher and faster—so high and fast that the theater could no longer contain them! Off they went, bursting out into the streets of Piggie-Town like naughty pogo sticks.

The Wiz Pig drew his wizard's hat over his eyes.

"Oh dear, oh dear, oh dear," he said. "I can never do anything right."

Muffin felt a pang. She sometimes felt that way in Piggie-Town, too. "It's all right. We'll figure it— ZIGGY! Will you stop bouncing for one second so I can think?"

6

ZIGGY AND THE MOST DELICIOUS PASSWORD!!

Ziggy could have kept bouncing forever, but Muffin was tapping her bunny foot *very* sternly.

On top of that, the Wiz Pig looked SO sad. Magicians shouldn't look sad!

"Is there something wrong with your wand?" she asked. The celery stalk had seen better days: it was all brown and floppy.

The Wiz Pig grabbed at his hat in dismay. "You're right! My wand should be crisp and green, with a silver star at the end! It's lost its sparkle!"

"Maybe that's why the spell didn't work," said Muffin. "Wiz Pig, when do you last remember seeing the sparkle?"

The Wiz Pig's brow furrowed. "Back at my magic castle. It was *definitely* there when I brewed my magical dandelion tea. And put on my magical knickerbockers. And read my magical newspaper."

"Is there anyone else who might have seen what happened?" asked Muffin.

The Wiz Pig drooped. "Not a single soul. I live all alone."

What an awful thought! The Wiz Pig must be so lonely without a hutch-mate!

Muffin's bunny ears flopped as she nodded. "Let's retrace your steps, beginning at the magic castle."

Ziggy bounced up and down. (Oops, too high.) They were going to a magic castle!! The best kind of castle!!

Muffin cleared her throat. "Given how we look right now, I suppose the best way to travel is . . . in a train."

A train! Finally, Muffin was coming around to the wonders of piggie public transit!

"I'll be the engine," said Muffin. "Ziggy, you can be the caboose."

Woo-hoo! Ziggy loved being the caboose!

"Wiz Pig, you're in the middle," directed Muffin.

The Wiz Pig squeezed in between them.

"Hold on tight!" cried Ziggy.

After a few false starts (bunny trains were harder to control than piggie trains), they bounced out of the theater and into Piggie-Town. This was fun!

"That way." The Wiz Pig pointed out a grand castle high up on a distant hill.

Were those carrot turrets? And turnip domes?

And rhubarb parapets?! (That was a Muffin word, but Ziggy loved it because it sounded like the noise her trumpet made.)

"There's no time to waste." Muffin nudged the Wiz Pig and Ziggy along. Off they bounced, gaining height with each leap. Ziggy wished they could stop at the disco dandelions and the confetti trees (and Mr. Cuddlecake's Bakery). But they were on a mission!

"We're here!" cried Muffin.

After a *gazillion* jumps, they'd landed outside the most ginormous potato-skin door Ziggy had ever seen. All right, the only potato-skin door she'd ever seen.

The Wiz Pig wrung his paws. "I should warn you that the door's been a bit funny since the previous owner lost the key. It asks the most *difficult* questions before it lets me in. I was once stuck out here all night because I

couldn't remember the name of the guinea pig constellation."

"Cavia Porcellus Major," grumbled the door. "Everyone knows that."

(Ziggy had not known that! But she did now!)

"Anyway, it's so nice to have someone here to help!" The Wiz Pig knocked on the door.

The door looked them up and down, then creaked impressively.

"If you wish to pass, riddle me this: What is the best midnight snack in all of Piggie-Town?"

Muffin shuddered. She never ate after dusk. "A sip of water to avoid an upset tummy?"

"Wrong!" cried the door. "Extremely wrong!"

The Wiz Pig nibbled his wand. "I know this. I do. A . . . juicy Roma tomato?"

"Appallingly wrong! Woe! Woe is me!"

Ziggy thought very, very hard. So hard that time seemed to stop.

"Super Rainbow Salad Pizza," she said finally.

The door regarded her for a moment. "I'd never even thought of that. What a brilliant mind!"

The door swung open.

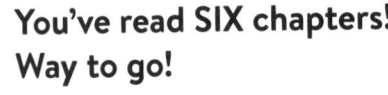

You've read SIX chapters! Way to go!

7

MUFFIN AND THE DIGNIFIED SEARCH PARTY

Super Rainbow Salad Pizza? This castle was not to be trusted!

Once inside, Muffin reconsidered.

All right, so the front door had terrible taste in food. But the castle was magnificent (and very tidy). The whole thing was built from neatly chopped vegetables stuck together with potato starch.

Wide corridors led off in all directions, and there were maps above every intersection. How orderly!

"I get lost easily," explained the Wiz Pig. "I have the memory of a goldfish."

"Me too!" exclaimed Ziggy. (She really did.) "Is that why you have that WONDERFUL portrait? So you don't forget what you look like?"

Muffin pushed her bunny ears out of her eyes. Above them was an enormous and terribly blotchy portrait of the Wiz Pig. The paint had run down over the frame, and there was a smeared section where someone had cleaned off a food spatter.

"It looks JUST like you!" said Ziggy. Then she paused. "Except they got your wand wrong.

It's all green and glowy in the picture!"

"That's what it *should* look like," said the Wiz Pig.

He pointed to what Muffin had taken to be a smudge. Squinting, she saw it *was* a wand—just an abstract one. It was a crisp green line with a sparkling silver star at its tip.

Now at least they knew what they were looking for.

"Let's form a search party," said Muffin. "We'll . . ."

"SEARCH PARTY!!" shrieked Ziggy.

Muffin sighed. "Not that kind of party, Ziggy."

The Wiz Pig pulled a party horn out of his hat. "Here. Take this. Maybe it'll help."

"MAGIC!!" squealed Ziggy.

"Just a secret pocket," admitted the Wiz Pig.

"Clever," said Muffin. (Muffin had a soft spot for pockets. Who didn't?)

"That's magic to me!" added Ziggy. "Let's go find this sparkle!!"

"Just a second." Muffin was trying to get a sense of the castle layout and the most efficient way to explore it.

Boing! TOOT! Boing! Off Ziggy went.

The Wiz Pig shrugged and followed after her.

"Here, sparkle!" echoed Ziggy's voice from some far-off corridor.

"Where are you, sparkle?" boomed the Wiz Pig from the opposite end of the castle.

Muffin was on her own. At least that meant she could do things in an organized manner.

She turned to the first door in front of her.

Maybe she'd skip that one for now.

You've read SEVEN chapters! Time to popcorn!

8

ZIGGY AND THE CASTLE KARAOKE SINGER!!

This was the best treasure hunt of all time! (And Ziggy had done a lot of treasure hunts.) The castle was so fun and magical and bouncy! And it was full of rooms that Ziggy was absolutely going to beg Muffin to add to their hutch when they got back. She had great fun sticking her nose in all of them.

There'd been no sign of the sparkle, but she'd found some spectacular souvenirs.

There was a velvety beret, a stunningly swishy cape, and a hatpin made from a parsley sprig.

She munched on the sprig as she posed in front of a mirror. (Now she was in the Hall of Mirrors.) A whole herd of bunny-eared Ziggys posed back!

This was amazing! Ziggy led the other Ziggys in an aerobics routine. High step, high step, side to side . . . and grapevine!

Ziggy blinked. So did the other Ziggys. What was she meant to be doing again?

Above her, in the Nook of Natural Light, a firefly sparked.

Of course! She was looking for the magical sparkle!

Ziggy closed her eyes and let her instincts guide her.

She nosed her way into a room labeled Parlor of Friends. Inside was the most magnificent sweet potato table—imagine the time it would have taken to carve! On the table was a lustrous tea set that Ziggy wanted so *badly* to play with. But what if she broke it? And what if all the teddies sitting around the table saw?

Something about the room made Ziggy feel sad. Why *were* all those teddies sitting around

the table, anyway? Wasn't this the Parlor of Friends? The Wiz Pig surely had a *bajillion* piggie friends he could invite to his fabulous castle! Who wouldn't want to visit a castle?! Especially with the way the wind moaned and howled through its corridors like someone singing a song.

Ziggy's bunny ears pricked. (What a funny feeling!) Someone *was* singing a song!

Karaoke! Ziggy LOVED karaoke! She *had* to find the singer so she could join in!

She was so glad she was wearing her amazingly artistic beret!!

9

MUFFIN AND THE CASE OF UNMISTAKABLE IDENTITY

Top hat. Fedora. Ascot. Fez.

How many formal hats could a single Sparkle Pig possibly need? How was anyone supposed to catalog them all?

Muffin sat down on a hatbox and massaged her bunny feet. This search was taking far too long. And these *ears*! They were constantly in the way. How did bunnies manage?

Hold on. What was that?

Muffin's bunny ears were picking up a song about . . . *rutabagas*?

But wait. Something about the rutabaga song was ringing a bell. A tuneless bell, but a bell nonetheless.

Muffin hauled herself off the hatbox and scurried up the exit ramp, following the song left, then right, then loop the loop. Finally, she arrived at the Gallery of Spell Books (not to be confused with the Gallery of Spelling Books).

WHUMP!

Ziggy arrived at the same moment.

"Muffin, fancy seeing you here!!" Ziggy tooted her party horn. "I didn't know you liked karaoke!"

"I don't!" huffed Muffin. "I'm following a lead."

Muffin pushed the door open. Inside was a rather undignified sight: the Wiz Pig was rummaging through teetering stacks of books, *singing* at the top of his piggie lungs.

Muffin cleared her throat. The Wiz Pig jumped, then pulled his hat down over his face.

"I'm sorry if I disturbed you," he mumbled. "I sing to fill the silence, you see."

"Singing is an amazing way to fill silence!"

exclaimed Ziggy. "Talking is, too!!"

Muffin had almost forgotten what silence was.

"Are you lonely, Wiz Pig?" pressed Ziggy. "Is that why you have tea parties with your teddies?"

The Wiz Pig blinked. His jaw wobbled, the same way Ziggy's did when Muffin asked her not to bathe in their drinking water.

"Yes," admitted the Wiz Pig. His tears fell on the book he held.

Poor Wiz Pig! Muffin dabbed at his soggy face with a hanky she'd borrowed from the Room of Handkerchiefs (Formal).
Then she dabbed at the book, too. Phew, just in time to stop the ink from running!

"If you teach me the words to your song, I'll sing with you," said Ziggy.

The Wiz Pig sniffled. "That's very kind. It begins, well . . ."

"It's so easy to root for rutabagas.

"They're always, always on the beet.

"I love to turn it up for rutabagas

"'Cause rutabagas are so neat!"

"That's . . . all I have," admitted the Wiz Pig.

A rutabaga song. Hadn't Granny Pig said that Fred sang funny rutabaga songs? (Although was there any other type?)

It couldn't be, could it?

Muffin, in a very un-Muffiny manner, blurted: "Wiz Pig . . . are you *Fred*?"

You've read NINE chapters! Let's do a happy dance!

10

ZIGGY AND THE MASTER OF DISGUISE!!

Ziggy jumped so high from astonishment that she bonked her head on the decorative ceiling.

The Wiz Pig was Fred? And Fred was the Wiz Pig? They were both each other?! What a trick! What sorcery!

As Ziggy gaped in wonderment, the Wiz Pig removed his hat. THEN HIS BEARD!!!

Ziggy squeaked in terror. "Wiz Pig! I mean, Wiz Fred! I mean, Fred Pig! Are you all right?

Do you need first aid?"

"I'm perfectly fine, Ziggy," said the beardless Wiz Pig. He sighed. "And . . . perfectly normal. Muffin is right. I'm not the Wiz Pig. I'm not even a Sparkle Pig. I'm just a standard, run-of-the-hutch guinea pig."

"Like us!!" Ziggy was SO relieved. She LOVED being a regular, run-of-the-hutch guinea pig! And now it turned out the Wiz Pig

was one, too! AMAZING!!

"How did you end up here? As a magician inhabiting a very impressive castle?" asked Muffin. (Muffin asked such good questions.)

Fred propped his paws up against a stack of spell books. "Well, when I first visited Piggie-Town, I was bespelled by it. It's so magical and so *sparkly*!"

"SO sparkly," agreed Ziggy.

"When the last Wiz Pig retired to Hamster Heath, I decided to stay on and look after the castle," Fred went on. "But I was worried that the Sparkle Pigs wouldn't like a regular piggie moving in on their turf. So I've been keeping my identity a secret."

A secret identity! Ziggy had always wanted to have a secret identity!

But the way Fred talked about it, it didn't sound fun at all.

"But, Fred," Ziggy said, "the Sparkle Pigs talk about you *all* the time. They'd be so excited to know that you're here!"

Fred seemed to brighten. "Really?"

"Really," said Muffin. "And honesty is always the best policy."

"It is!" exclaimed Ziggy. (She definitely planned to tell Muffin all about the secret hole she'd nibbled in their hutch. Really. Truly.)

Fred brightened again. But *actually* this time. The whole room filled with brilliant, sparkly light. It was so bright that Ziggy had to hide behind her bunny ears!

This is what it must be like to be a star! (Ziggy had always wanted to be a star!)

After a moment, the bright light gathered itself. It perched on the tip of Fred's wand.

"FRED!" shouted Ziggy. "Your sparkle is BACK!"

You've read TEN chapters! You're a super sparkly star!

11

MUFFIN AND THE END OF THE BUNNY BUSINESS

Fred's sparkle was indeed back. In fact, it was so bright that it lit up every dusty corner in the castle. (Muffin would have to give Fred some cleaning tips.)

"I feel like myself again!" exclaimed Fred. He puffed up, holding himself with confidence.

Muffin smiled. "When you hid yourself, your sparkle went into hiding as well."

"BUT NOW YOU'RE BOTH BACK!!"

squealed Ziggy. "WHAT AN INCREDIBLE COINCIDENCE!!"

"It's not..." began Muffin. She sighed. There was no point explaining. "Fred, could you turn everyone back now?"

Fred reached for his wizardy hat and wizardy beard.

Muffin took her place at the front of the piggie train, and Ziggy at the rear. Holding Fred between them, they bounced back to the

Piggie-Town Theater.

They arrived to a scene of bunny chaos. But slightly less energetic chaos than before. Several bunnified Sparkle Pigs hopped slowly down the road, using bunches of carrots to weigh themselves down. Others clung to lampposts.

"I'm not fit enough for all this bouncing," moaned Scooter. "My legs are killing me!"

"It's almost over," promised Muffin. "But I do need you to put on your conductor's hat.

We need a train to get everyone back inside the theater . . . and quickly."

Scooter didn't need to be told twice.

"All right, party piggies!" cried Scooter. "All aboard the piggie train! Let's bounce this party back inside!"

But the Sparkle Pigs weren't known for following instructions. They continued to vault and hop around, smooshing Chatter's lovely carrot garden and rebounding off the floofy shopfront of the Piggie Wiggery.

Until . . .

TOOT! Ziggy gave an ear-splitting blast on her party horn.

The Sparkle Pigs stopped in their bouncy tracks.

Groaning about sore paws and aching backs, the exhausted piggies skipped their way into a (relatively) orderly piggie train. The ushers helped everyone take their seats (or at least get close).

Fred scurried up to the stage, hiding his face beneath his hat. He narrowly missed tripping over his wizardy beard.

"Wiz Pig! Turn us *back*!"

"No more bunny business!"

Fred cleared his throat. The lights dimmed.

Then *FFFFT!* He whipped off his hat and beard.

"He just pulled off his FACE!" squealed Mr. Cuddlecake.

"Fake beard," Muffin reassured the Sparkle Pigs. "It's a fake beard."

Fred blinked, squinting in the bright stage lights. He seemed so small.

Muffin's heart went out to him. She didn't like having everyone's attention on her, either.

"I'm sorry for deceiving you, friends." There was a wobble in Fred's voice. "I just love Piggie-Town and the Sparkle

Pigs *so much*. I wasn't sure that you'd accept plain old me as the Wiz Pig."

There was silence as the Sparkle Pigs tried to make sense of this announcement. Then . . .

"Fred?" murmured Granny Pig. "Is that you, Fred? Oh, how we've missed you!"

"The Wiz Pig was Fred all along?" cried Scooter. "What an extraordinary illusion!"

"An illusion only the Wiz Pig could manage!" added Granny Pig.

"Fred's back! Fred's back!" chanted the Sparkle Pigs.

Fred beamed. The sparkle on his wand gleamed proudly.

"I'm going to turn you all back," he promised. "Are you ready? Say . . . cheese!"

"CHEESE!" shouted the Sparkle Pigs.

Fred raised his wand.

FLASH!

Everything suddenly seemed *dazzlingly* bright. But that was because Muffin's bunny ears were no longer in her eyes. In fact, they were no longer on her head.

Muffin reached for her crinkly piggie ears and almost whooped with joy.

"PIGGIE PAWS!" cried Ziggy. "I have piggie paws! I LOVE having piggie paws!"

All around them the Sparkle Pigs popcorned and wheeked happily.

Fluffina wobbled back onto the stage (it took a while to get used to being back on piggie paws).

"Anyone who's attended a Piggie Parade knows that no one does a detour like the Sparkle Pigs!" She laughed. "But we're back on track now, and the talent show must go on!"

"Time to shine! Time to shine!" chanted the Sparkle Pigs.

Muffin slid down in her chair. She was fine with the talent show continuing, just so long as she wasn't up next.

12

ZIGGY AND THE GRAND FINALE!!

Ziggy was up next!! She'd thought super long and hard, and she'd finally narrowed down her talents to just two!!

"Ziggy's first talent is . . . styling!" said Fluffina approvingly. (She was also very stylish!) "Dim the lights!"

Ziggy cleared her throat. She'd never walked a piggiewalk, but she knew she could do it.

She threw her cape over her shoulders and STRUTTED.

She was strong. She was *fierce*. She was INVINCIBLE. Like a POSSUM.

"Oooh!" went the Sparkle Pigs. "Ahhhh!"

Muffin gaped. She was so impressed she was speechless!

But Ziggy wasn't done yet! She whipped off her beret and cape and flung them into the crowd.

(Granny Pig caught them in a truly epic outfielding move—what a classic catch!)

Fluffina waited for the applause to die down. "And now for Ziggy's second talent: the dance routine!"

A flower trombone started blasting, then a tuba! Ziggy's brass band friends were playing her song!

Ziggy twirled. She sashayed. She cha-cha-chaed. She even tangoed!! It was just like in her dream!

All the piggies danced along in their seats. When Ziggy gave her final bow, they applauded so thunderously they sounded like actual thunder!

"Careful, Ziggy, or you'll bring the roof down," yelled Mr. Cuddlecake.

Muffin looked alarmed, but Ziggy was sure it was fine. The Sparkle Pigs were excellent engineers!

"You were AMAZING!" whispered Granny Pig as Ziggy flounced back to her seat.

"And next we have Muffin!" Fluffina squinted at her cue card. "With . . . a mystery talent!"

Muffin shuffled out, blinking under the spotlight. Everyone had a talent but her. Why, even Fred had his funny rutabaga song. Muffin only had her cleaning . . .

"Poem!" she blurted. "I'm going to recite a cleaning poem!"

"HOORAY!" squealed Ziggy. She didn't know much about poetry. But she did know that she was Muffin's number one fan!!

Muffin cleared her throat. The microphone whined with feedback.

"'An Ode to Cleaning,'" Muffin began.

"Who's Ode?" whispered Scooter.

"Oh, I am a tidy piggie," began Muffin, *"I polish, scrub, and clean. Turning disarray to sweet bouquet . . . I am a hygiene queen!"*

It was the most wonderful cleaning poem Ziggy had ever heard!

It rhymed! It had rhythm! It had a *queen*!! It gave Ziggy warm fuzzies thinking about their lovely nesting box!

"BRAVO!" bellowed Ziggy. "BRAVO!"

Muffin caught her eye and smiled.

Ziggy's enthusiasm roused the other piggies (this was another of Ziggy's special talents). One by one they began clapping. The smattering of claps turned into a whole round of applause, and then some floor stomping! Hiding shyly behind her puffy sleeve, Muffin scurried off the stage.

Fluffina had reached the end of her list of performers. But

before she could begin her closing speech, Fred stepped forward. He was carrying a butternut squash guitar! "May I? If it's all right to go up twice."

"There's no such thing as too much Fred, Fred!" yelled Granny Pig.

Fred strummed his guitar and stepped out onto the stage.

"This is a little ditty I wrote about rutabagas," he began. "It goes a little something like . . .

"It's so easy to root for rutabagas.

"They're always, always on the beet.

"I love to turn it up for rutabagas

"'Cause rutabagas are so neat!"

The crowd. Went. Wild. (Especially Ziggy.)

It took a while for the cheering and whooping to subside.

Finally, Fluffina clacked back onstage, an envelope in her piggie paw. Opening it, she flashed a dazzling grin.

"The winner is . . ."

(A watermelon drumroll rumbled through the theater.)

". . . everyone! You get a ribbon. You get a ribbon. Everyone gets a ribbon!"

Ziggy squealed and wrapped Muffin up in a super squishy hug. She'd never won a ribbon before!!

And from the stunned look on her hutchmate's face, neither had Muffin.

You've read TWELVE chapters! You get a ribbon, too!

13

MUFFIN AND THE PERFECTLY PIGGIE ENDING

Muffin clutched her ribbon. It was so impeccably *blue*.

But that wasn't all that caught her attention. Off to stage left, a familiar glowing door had appeared. It was time to go home.

"Can we stay just a teensy bit longer?" pleaded Ziggy. "Fred's making up another song. He's almost found a rhyme for orange!"

Clonk. Fred played a tuneless chord.

Muffin grimaced.

"Just think, he'll have it perfected by the next time we visit." Muffin held out a paw for Ziggy. "Let's show the Sparkle Pigs our one-of-a-kind magical disappearing act."

Ziggy beamed. "ANOTHER special talent!"

Paw in paw, Muffin and Ziggy waved goodbye and stepped through the door into a pool of dazzling light.

FLUMP.

Home tidy home. Muffin hung her ribbon neatly on the wall.

"What a great landing!" squealed Ziggy, who had skidded the length of the hutch. Her ribbon went flying, landing upside down in their food dish. "And what a perfect spot for my ribbon!"

Home untidy home. Muffin raised her paws, then realized she'd been about to smooth back her bunny ears!

"Muffin, I saw that," squealed Ziggy.

"Those ears *were* good for hiding behind when everything got too much," admitted Muffin.

"And I'll miss my bouncy feet!" added Ziggy. "ALTHOUGH, LOOK AT THIS!"

Ziggy popcorned like a piggie pinball.

"That *is* great," admitted Muffin. "Being a piggie is its own special brand of fun."

"I wouldn't change our piggieness for the world," agreed Ziggy. "Well, maybe for one of Mr. Cuddlecake's double-decker carrot dream cheesecakes."

"Carrot dream . . . cheesecake?" mumbled Muffin, who was already halfway asleep. She was so tired she didn't even need to count bell peppers!

Luckily, she held on just long enough that she didn't miss the twins stopping by to say good night.

"Look how cute they are, all snuggled up together!" said Sophia.

"Hang on. Where did those ribbons come from?" asked Jackson.

"Don't look at me," said Sophia. "Although

these two are *definitely* a couple of prize-winning piggies."

Jackson chuckled. "You're right. They deserve all the blue ribbons in the whole wide world for being so adorable."

Muffin opened an eye and stole a glance at Ziggy, who was grinning mischievously. If only the twins knew how they'd *really* won the ribbons!

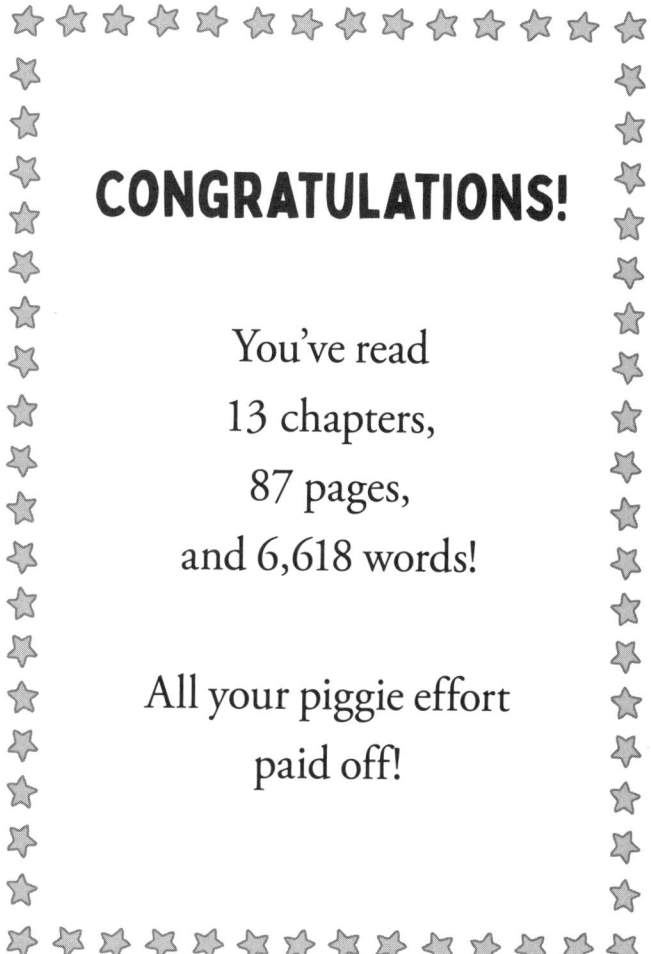

ABOUT THE AUTHOR

Kit Holliday is the pen name for Stephanie Campisi, an Aussie author living in the US (which puts her much closer to the natural habitat of guinea pigs and capybaras—hooray!). She loves sparkly things, silly jokes, and carrot cake. When she's not dreaming up magical worlds, she spends her time going on adventures with her fabulous family and her cheeky dog.

ABOUT THE ILLUSTRATORS

The team behind Dizzy Devil Designs is **Francesca Brylewski** and **David Brylewski**. They met while studying at Newport Film School. After graduation, they both moved to London and went on to have very successful careers in film and television animation before forming their own illustration company. Now living in Dorset with their two grown-up kids, they continue to work together creating fun children's illustrations in both traditional and digital mediums.